The Smile Shop

Published by
PEACHTREE PUBLISHING COMPANY INC.
1700 Chattahoochee Avenue
Atlanta, Georgia 30318-2112
www.peachtree-online.com

Text and illustrations © 2020 by Satoshi Kitamura

First published in Great Britain in 2019 by Scallywag Press Ltd
10 Sutherland Row, London SW1V 4JT
First United States version published in 2021 by Peachtree Publishing Company Inc.

The illustrations were created with pen, ink, watercolor, and gouache.

Printed in October 2020 in China
10 9 8 7 6 5 4 3 2 1
First Edition
ISBN: 978-1-68263-255-0

Cataloging-in-Publication Data is available from the Library of Congress

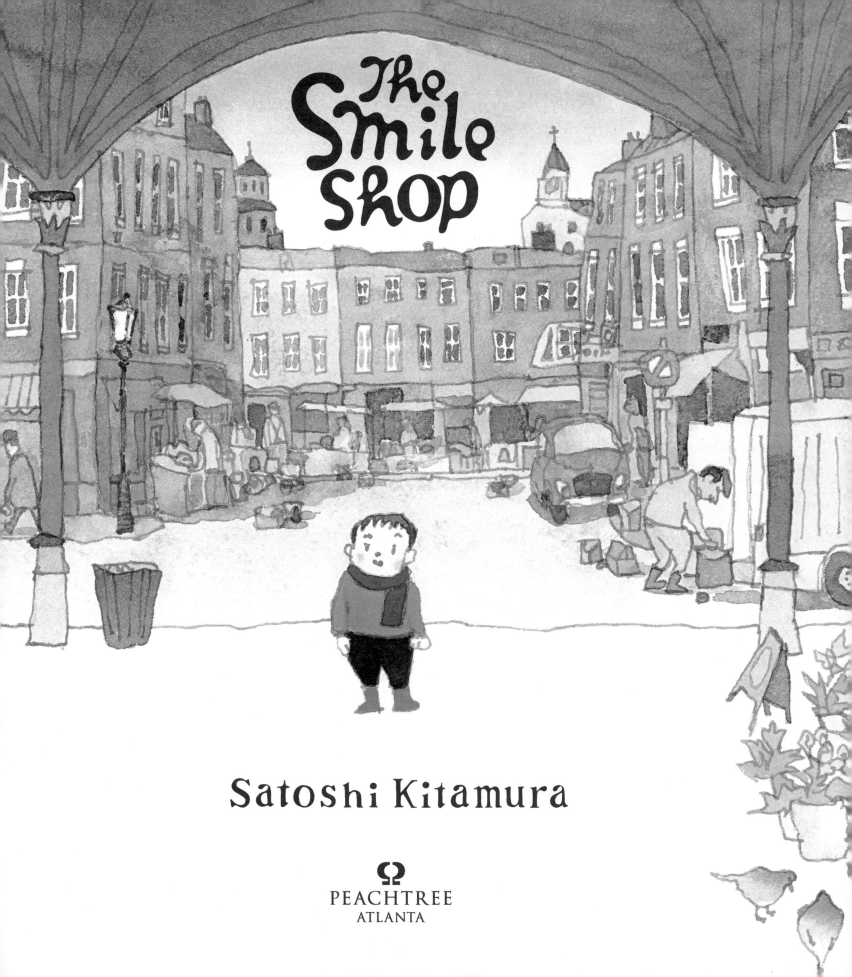

The Smile Shop

Satoshi Kitamura

PEACHTREE
ATLANTA

I'm so excited!

I have saved all my pocket money
and today I'm going to buy myself
something for the very first time . . .

The market is very busy.

There are so many shops and stalls,
and such wonderful colors . . .

and tempting smells!

That apple pie looks tasty.

I wonder which clock is telling the right time?

Oh, what a beautiful
little boat. It's quite
expensive, though.

Wow!
I can make a sound on this horn!

I like this hat!
It suits me head to toe.

Now I must decide
what to buy.

What? Oh no!

My money has gone down the drain!

Only one coin
is left . . .

I haven't enough
to buy anything now.

"SMILE"?
Is this a smile shop?
Do they sell smiles here?

A smile is probably what I need,
although I don't feel like smiling . . .

"Excuse me," I say to the man behind the counter. "I have very little money but could I buy a smile, please? A little one, perhaps?"

"I'm afraid we don't sell smiles here, sir," he replies.

"But I thought you were a Smile Shop," I whisper.

"Well, we call our store 'Smile,'" the man goes on,
"but a smile is not something that money can buy . . ."
He stops talking and looks at me.

And then . . .

"A smile is really something you can only exchange and share!"

And he smiles a big smile.

So I smile, too!

The man takes a
picture of me smiling
and he gives the
photo to me.

We exchange smiles again
and wave goodbye.

And I see that everyone
on the street is smiling.
The whole world
is smiling . . .

. . . smiling with me.